MAUDE

The Not-So-Noticeable Shrimpton

lauren child

illustrated by

trisha krauss

CANDLEWICK PRESS

For Ferdi, Wardi,
Tess and Hector,
with love,
Trisha

For the most
noticeable Delfina,
with love,
Lauren

First U.S. edition 2013

Library of Congress Cataloging-in-Publication Data is available.

Library of Congress Catalog Card Number pending

ISBN 978-0-7636-6515-9

13 14 15 16 17 18 LEO 10 9 8 7 6 5 4 3 2 1

Printed in Heshan, Guangdong, China

This book was typeset in Cambria and Arial Black.

Candlewick Press, 99 Dover Street, Somerville, Massachusetts 02144

visit us at www.candlewick.com

The SHRIMPTON family!

Wherever the Shrimptons went, people **noticed** them.
They were **so talented, so eccentric, so larger** than life . . .
you just **couldn't miss them** even if you wanted to.

The Shrimptons hated to be *missed.*

They spent a great deal of time
and trouble making sure that
they never went unnoticed.

Mrs. Shrimpton created
flamboyant hats
from feathers, fruit, and fur.
Her latest had a live peacock
positioned perkily
on top.

Mrs. Shrimpton's hats were real head-turners.

Mr. Shrimpton's mustache was
so **long** and so *twirly*
that butterflies liked to
perch on it.

It was quite a statement as mustaches go.

Penelope Shrimpton was *exceedingly* beautiful.

She could **STOP** traffic just by walking out of the house. She caused frightful street jams.

People *gasped* when they saw her turn the corner.

Hector Shrimpton was a mesmerizing mover —
toe-tappingly mesmerizing.
He wore his tap shoes in math class,
at tap class, and everywhere
in between.

$$4\frac{2}{3} + 7\frac{1}{9} = 4 + \frac{2}{3} + 7 + 9$$
$$= 11 + \frac{2}{3} + \frac{1}{9}$$
$$= \frac{99}{9} + \frac{6}{9} + \frac{1}{9}$$
$$= \frac{106}{9}$$

**It was
heel-toe,
heel-toe
wherever he went.**

Constance Shrimpton had
a voice like *music*.
An **"um"** or an **"ah"** from her could get
all the birds in the trees a-twitter.

Wardo Shrimpton, **HA HA HA** (excuse me while I clutch my sides),
was **so funny** that if he even *thought* a funny thought,
he laughed out loud — and he was
always thinking
funny thoughts.

He was a
laugh a minute,
and no one found him
funnier
than he did.

All except, that is, for Maude Shrimpton.

Unlike Penelope, when Maude crossed the street, she had to **dodge** cars.

She moved so
inconspicuously
that when she
performed in her
school play,
people thought she
was part of the scenery.

Her voice was so small
that not even the Shrimptons'
collection of unusual dogs
could hear her.

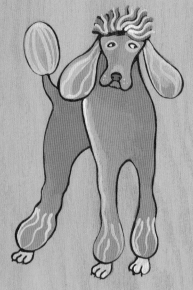

And **dogs,** as you know,
have *exceptional* hearing.

No matter what she wore,
Maude just seemed to *merge*, to fade, to disappear.

She was what you might call a *blender*.

People often remarked, "What a shame it is for the Shrimptons that their middle child isn't more . . .

something.

She doesn't seem to have a talent for *anything,* and it is so **important** to be good at, well, at least one thing. **She's just so bland."**

All in all, Maude Shrimpton
stuck out like a very sore thumb.

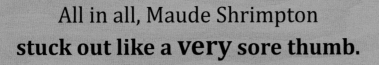

**Well, she would have if you had
actually ever noticed she was there.**

"A goldfish," said Maude.

"What a *marvelous* idea," exclaimed her father. "A **GIANT** carp or a **whale**! Something enormous."

"I want a goldfish," said Maude.

"Yes, yes, yes," said her mother. "Something golden, like a *phoenix*."

"Just a goldfish," said Maude.

So, on her birthday,
Maude Shrimpton,
with great excitement,
unwrapped her
present.

Maude found it quite *embarrassing* to leave
the house
with a **TIGER**
in tow.

Everyone **looked** at them.

But all the other Shrimptons simply *loved* how people **stared**

as they strolled along the boulevard with a **GIANT CAT.**

The tiger could do wonderful tricks.
My, was he eye-catching.

Those **daring** leaps, those **impossible** feats. Such **stripy** stripes, such **long, sharp** claws, such **pointy** teeth, such a **BIG** appetite. . . .

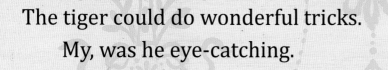

And that's the thing to
remember about tigers:
they do get **very** hungry.

And when a tiger is hungry . . .
it is VERY hungry indeed.

And so it was that one Tuesday in August, Mrs. Shrimpton returned from shopping to hear a terrible **ROAR!**

"What's that about?" she said.

"We have run out of tiger food," said Maude.

"Oh, dear!"
shouted Mr. Shrimpton,
running to the pantry.

"Feed it muffins!
Feed it rolls!
Feed it anything!"
cried Penelope.

But it was
TOO late. . . .

"**RUN!**" shrieked Mrs. Shrimpton, holding on to her panicking peacock hat.

YUM, thought the tiger.

"**Hide!**" shouted Mr. Shrimpton, his mustache all a-quiver.

I Married Adventure

"Disappear," whispered Penelope, blinking her dazzling blue eyes.

Y U M
Y U M,
thought
the tiger.

"Quiet!" gasped Constance, setting all the birds a-tweet.

"Tiptoe," stuttered Hector, tip-tapping his shiny shoes.

"HA HA HA!" giggled Wardo, trying to see the funny side.

YUM YUM YUM, thought the tiger.

And Maude just stood completely still.
Can YOU see her?

**Sometimes, just sometimes,
not being noticeable is the
very best talent of all.**